This book belongs to

DUDLEY SCHOOLS
LIBRARY SERVICE

FREDERICK WARNE

Published by the Penguin Group

Penguin Books Ltd., 80 Strand, London WC2R 0RL, England
Penguin Group (USA) Inc., 375 Hudson Street, New York, New York 10014, USA
Penguin Group (Australia), 250 Camberwell Road, Camberwell, Victoria 3124, Australia (a division of Pearson Australia Group Pty. Ltd.)
Penguin Group (Canada), 90 Eglinton Avenue East, Suite 700, Toronto, Ontario M4P 2Y3, Canada (a division of Pearson Penguin Canada Inc.)
Penguin Books India Pvt. Ltd., 11 Community Centre, Panchsheel Park, New Delhi—110 017, India
Penguin Group (NZ), 67 Apollo Drive, Rosedale, Auckland 0632, New Zealand (a division of Pearson New Zealand Ltd.)
Penguin Books (South Africa) (Pty.) Ltd., 24 Sturdee Avenue, Rosebank, Johannesburg 2196, South Africa

Penguin Books Ltd., Registered Offices: 80 Strand, London WC2R 0RL, England
001-1 2 3 4 5 6 7 8 9 10

Copyright © Frederick Warne & Co., 2012

Manufactured in China

With special thanks to Mark Burgess and Richard Dungworth.

The Tale of a Silly Little Duck

F. WARNE & CO

This is the story of a farmyard duck who wanted, more than anything, to hatch her own eggs.

Here she is, LOOK, Jemima Puddle-duck, the loveliest of ducks, with such fine white feathers.

But poor Jemima!
Every time she laid some eggs
the farmer's wife gave them to
the hens to hatch instead.

This upset Jemima. Her sister-in-law, Mrs Rebecca Puddle-duck, thought she was being silly. 'I don't have the patience to sit on a nest for twenty-eight days!' she told Jemima. 'And neither do you!'

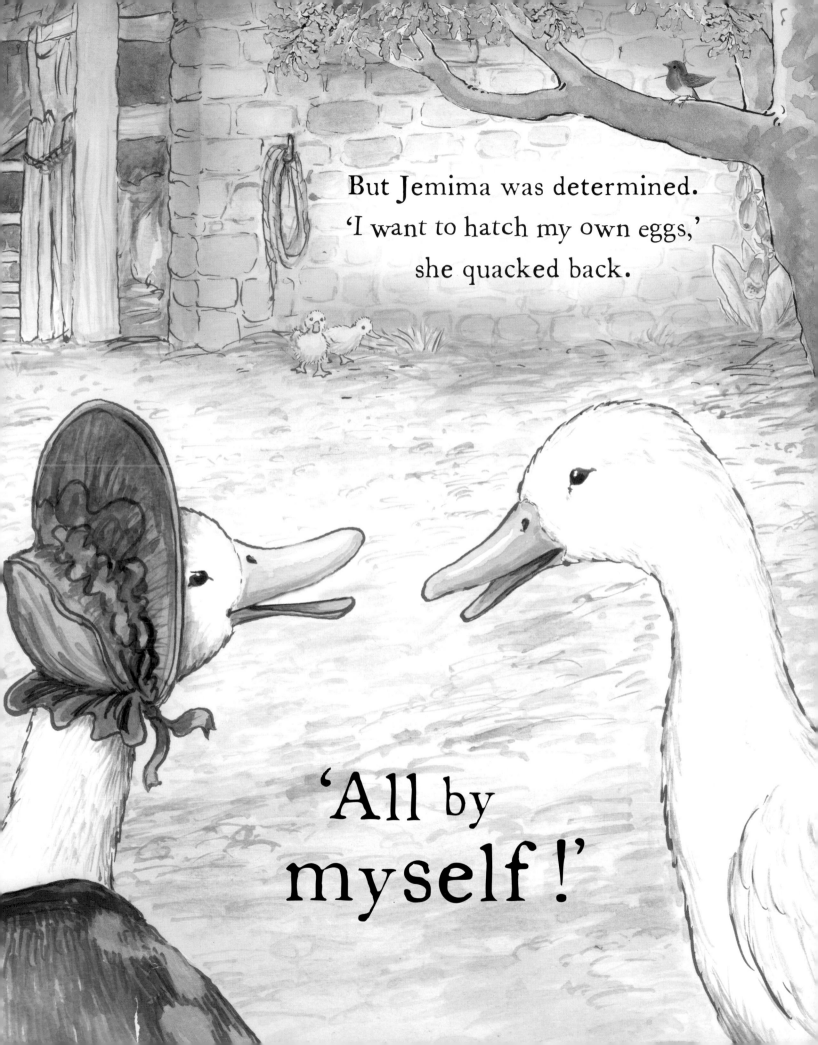

But Jemima was determined.
'I want to hatch my own eggs,'
she quacked back.

'All by
myself!'

So one fine spring afternoon Jemima set out – in her best bonnet and finest shawl, to find a secret place to lay her eggs.

pit-pat

paddle-pat

waddle-pat

pit-pat

She followed the cart track to the top of the hill.
From there, she could see a wood.

It looked like a safe, quiet spot.

Jemima decided to fly the rest of the way.
She wasn't terribly good at taking off.
But after a great deal of flapping...

...she was up, up and away!

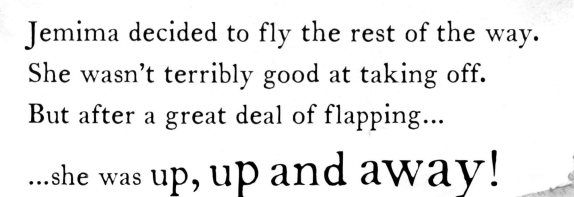

Jemima landed, rather heavily, in the middle of the wood.

She was not alone. Sitting
nearby was a smartly
dressed gentleman.

He had black, pointy ears,
sandy-coloured whiskers
and a long, bushy tail.

He appeared not
to notice Jemima.

RECIPE OF THE
DAY

SAGE AND ONION
STUFFING

WOODLAND NEWS

RABBIT
FOUND SAFE
AND WELL

WANTED

'Quack?' said Jemima Puddle-duck, with her head to one side. 'Quack?' The gentleman looked up and said, most politely, 'Madam, have you lost your way?'

Jemima thought the gentleman **very** charming
and **very** handsome – the sort of gentleman
a lady could trust. She told him all about
her search for a safe, dry nesting-place.

'How interesting!' said the sandy-whiskered gentleman.
'My own summer residence has a snug little woodshed.
It would be just the place!' he told Jemima. 'You would
not find my earth – my winter house, I mean – so convenient.'

He politely led Jemima to
a tumble-down shed and showed
her inside. To her surprise,
the little shed was full of feathers.

Jemima was soon too busy
making herself comfortable
to give much thought to why.

Here she is, LOOK,
Jemima Puddle-duck,
the most trusting of ducks,
on her snug, feathery nest.

Jemima visited her nest every afternoon, and
before long, had laid **nine fine white eggs**.
The bushy-tailed gentleman admired them greatly.
He counted them **every day**.

He was so very polite, he seemed almost sorry
to let Jemima go home each night.

'Tomorrow, I will begin to sit,' Jemima told
the gentleman one afternoon. 'And I shall not leave
my nest until all my eggs are hatched.'

'Madam,' he replied, 'Before you begin your hard work,
let us have a **dinner party!** Just the two of us!'

He asked Jemima to visit the farm garden and gather
some herbs – sage, thyme and parsley – for their feast.
He told her to bring some onions, as well.

It never crossed Jemima's simple
mind that parsley and thyme were
just the thing to add to an omelette.
Or that sage and onion made a tasty
stuffing – for roasted duck.

At the farm, Kep, a wise old dog, spotted Jemima carrying the onions. 'What are you doing, Jemima Puddle-duck?' he asked. Jemima told him of her woodland nest, and of the charming gentleman with the sandy whiskers.

Kep gave a knowing smile.
He insisted Jemima describe **exactly**
where the shed stood before he went on his way.

By the time Jemima had collected the herbs and onions, she was tired out. It was all she could do to carry them back to the wood.

Jemima found the foxy gentleman waiting at the shed. He was sniffing the air, and glancing about nervously.

He was **not** nearly as polite as before.
'Give me the herbs!' he snapped.
'And come into the house!'

But first, Jemima went into the shed
– feeling rather **alarmed** –
to check on her eggs.

She was even more frightened, when
she heard the sound of paws padding
past outside. The **most awful**
noises suddenly filled the air –
barking and howling.

When the terrible noises stopped, a wet,
black nose nudged open the woodshed door.
It was Kep. He had a bite on one ear,
and two fox-hound friends for company.

And the bushy-tailed gentleman?
Well, of him, nothing more
was seen or heard **ever** again.

After her narrow escape the farmer's wife let
Jemima keep her next batch of eggs.

She wasn't terribly good at keeping them warm.
But she did manage to hatch four.

All by herself!

Here she is, LOOK –
Jemima Puddle-duck,
the luckiest of ducks, with
four fluffy little Puddle-ducklings.

Aren't they sweet?

The End